PUZZLE ODYSSEY

First published in Great Britain in 2021 by Laurence King Publishing

1 3 5 7 9 10 8 6 4 2

A CIP catalog record for this book
is available from the British Library.

ISBN 978-1-91394-730-9

Printed and bound in China

Laurence King Publishing
An imprint of
Hachette Children's Group
Part of Hodder and Stoughton
Carmelite House
50 Victoria Embankment
London EC4Y 0DZ

An Hachette UK Company
www.hachette.co.uk
www.hachettechildrens.co.uk

www.laurenceking.com

PUZZLE ODYSSEY

An Epic Maze Adventure

Helen Friel & Ian Friel
Illustrations by Jesús Sotés

Laurence King Publishing

Contents

Welcome to my world, traveler...

I am Odysseus, King of Ithaca.
How would I describe myself? I hear you ask.
Clever? Yes.
Cunning? Definitely.
Heroic? Yup.
Kingly? Yes, well, it comes with the job.
Some people have other names for me, though.
"Trouble" is one of them…

Us Greeks live in many small kingdoms, around the Middle Sea.
To us, the sea is everything.
We live by it, sail on it, and sometimes die in it.
The rulers of our world are the gods, who live on Mount Olympus.
Fortunately, they all like me, from Father Zeus down.
Athena, goddess of wisdom, is my special protector.

Aah, actually, that's not *quite* true.
About all the gods liking me.
As you will see, Poseidon became my enemy.
And who is Poseidon? He's god of the sea.
And where do I spend a lot of my time?
In a ship, on the sea. Or in the sea, swimming for my life.

This book retells the tale of my *odyssey*, a fancy name
for the voyages I made with my men after we won
the Trojan War. All we wanted was to see our families
and homes again. As things turned out, various gods
and monsters had other ideas…

Can you overcome the challenges that follow,
as I once did, and get me home to my
beloved Queen Penelope?

**Can you ensure that
I return to Ithaca?**

Cast of Characters

Here are the humans, gods, goddesses,
and monsters you will find on our voyage.

The humans

And who is the most handsome of the humans?
Here's a clue: the name begins with "O."
And no, the answer is not "Odysseus' sailors,"
fine chaps though they were…

Odysseus,
King of Ithaca and hero (me!)

Penelope,
heroic Queen of Ithaca

Telemachus,
equally heroic
Prince of Ithaca

Odysseus' sailors

Eumaeus,
a pig-herder

The Lotus Eaters

The Laestrygonians,
cannibals

Nausicaa,
Princess of
the Phaeacians

Alcinous,
King of the Phaeacians

108 Suitors

Gods, goddesses, not-quite humans, and monsters

Zeus,
Father of the gods

Athena,
goddess of wisdom,
my Lady and protector

Aeolus,
god of the winds

Poseidon,
god of the sea

Hermes,
messenger of the gods

Helios,
the Sun-god

Circe,
goddess and witch

Calypso,
woman and goddess

Ino,
goddess

Polyphemus,
Cyclops

The Sirens,
songstresses
and monsters

Charybdis,
whirlpool-creating
monster

Scylla,
many-headed
monster

The spooks

Tiresias,
a prophet

Anticlea,
my mother

Thousands of other
ghosts… scary and dull
—quite a trick!

And not forgetting…

Argus the dog

7

Lotus, Sheep, and Cannibals!

S o this is where the story begins... I left Troy with many men and a fleet of twelve ships. Our first landfall was in an unknown country. We beached the ships, stocked up with water, and sat down for lunch. Afterwards, I sent three men inland to scout around. There they met the Lotus Eaters.

Don't get me wrong, the Lotus Eaters are lovely people, vegetarians one and all, wouldn't hurt a fly, but they gave my men some lotus fruit to eat. Tastes of honey, apparently. And makes you forget *everything* apart from wanting to eat more lotus fruit!

When my sailors failed to return, I set out with a search party. I found the missing men munching mouthfuls of fruit, idiot grins on their faces. I ordered them to come back with me, but they refused to budge. Ever tried dragging intoxicated, sobbing Greek sailors back to their ships? I don't recommend it. Once aboard, they had to be chained up under the rowing benches until they recovered. We rowed away as fast as we could.

The fleet next reached another unknown island, but this one was close to the coast of an inhabited country. I took a ship to the mainland, hoping to make friends. Big mistake. It proved to be the land of the Cyclopes. You can't make friends with the Cyclopes. They are smelly, one-eyed giants—but that's not even the bad bit. They are rude, crude, and they eat people!

To cut a long story short, my crew and I ended up imprisoned in a cave belonging to the Cyclops Polyphemus, with a huge stone blocking our way out. It turned out that Polyphemus liked Greek food, so he wolfed down four of my men.

What I did next was devious and cruel, but we were desperate. I tricked the Cyclops into getting drunk, and then blinded his single eye with a stake when he fell asleep. Polyphemus awoke in a screaming rage. He pushed the stone from the cave mouth, but plonked himself down there, his giant body blocking the exit. We were still trapped.

Then, I had another idea. The cave was full of the Cyclops' big, fleecy sheep. When Polyphemus let the animals out to graze the next morning, we hung on to their woolly bellies and escaped as they ambled past him. We got to the ship and out to sea, but—me and my big mouth—I couldn't resist yelling back at Polyphemus, to let him know just how I had fooled him. He chucked some big chunks of mountain in the direction of my voice and almost sank the ship!

Unfortunately for me, Polyphemus was a son of Poseidon, god of the sea. Poseidon found out about what I had done to the Cyclops and from that day onward he wanted me dead.

Our next landfall was Aeolia, home of kindly Aeolus, god of the winds. The less said about this, the better. Aeolus gave us a wind to carry us home, but my mischievous men squandered his gift and we got blown straight back to Aeolia. The god was furious. Humiliated, we rowed away across a windless sea.

Six days' hard rowing took us to a land called Laestrygonia. We found what appeared to be a good, safe harbour, surrounded by high cliffs, and so we dropped our anchors.

I sent a group of men inland, to explore. Two of them made it back, pursued by thousands of huge, hungry Laestrygonians. Why hungry? The Laestrygonians are cannibals, and had eaten most of my exploring party as an appetizer. They were now after the main course—the fleet! The cannibals stood on top of the cliffs, bombarding the ships with rocks. My men were killed and then skewered with harpoons.

My ship was just out of range of the Laestrygonians, and that gave us a chance to escape. I cut the cable, and shouted at my crew to row for dear life. We survived, though the rest of my sailors and ships were lost.

Could things get any worse?

The Lotus Eaters

Don't eat the lotus fruit! You'll forget everything and never make it home. Some of my men ate their fill and I had to drag them back aboard.

Find your way back to the ship through the flowers. You can move up, down, left, or right, but only one space at a time and only to a flower of the same colour OR shape as the one you are already standing on. Make sure you avoid the lotus flowers!

Tricking the Cyclops

Hanging on underneath a sheep to sneak past the blinded Polyphemus... Heroic? Maybe not. Clever? Definitely!

Find your way through the tunnels to the opening of the cave and sneak past the blinded Cyclops. Hang on tightly to that sheep!

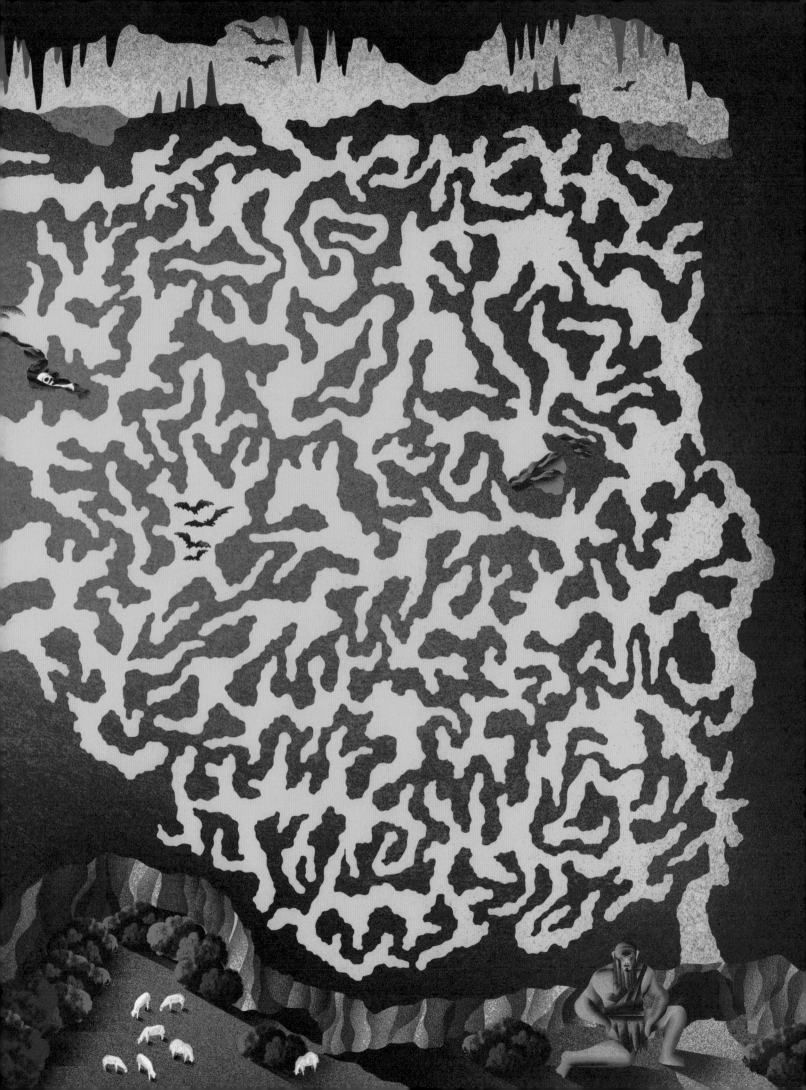

Attack of the Cannibals

The Laestrygonians killed most of my men here.
Only the crew of my ship and I escaped, because
we anchored out of range of their boulders.

Only Odysseus' ship is safe from
the cannibals. They can throw rocks
two squares up, down, left, or right.
Find Odysseus' ship so you can get
out of here!

Circe,
Spooks, and Scylla!

Where was I, traveler? Oh, yes—we were fleeing the cannibals, only one shipload of us left out of a dozen.

Still grieving for our dead friends, we eventually beached the ship on another strange island. It was the home of Circe—a beautiful and clever woman, but also a cunning and dangerous witch and *goddess*. I sent some men to spy out the land. They soon found Circe's palace, surrounded by unnaturally tame wolves and lions. She invited my men in for a snack. All very nice—except that the snack was poisoned and it wiped their memories. Circe then tapped each man with her wand and turned him into a pig.

One of my sailors hadn't eaten Circe's food, and scuttled back with the terrible news. I took up a bow and my great bronze sword and set off on a rescue mission, but really, it seemed hopeless. How do you overcome a sorceress? Luckily, the god Hermes intercepted me on the way (Hermes is one of my great-granddads: as

everyone knows, it's handy to have a god in the family). He told me that a Moly flower would act as an antidote to Circe's poison, and then explained how to defeat her.

I reached Circe's house, where I gobbled down the snack she offered me. It had no effect, and she found herself staring at the point of my sword. Goddess or not, Circe faced death. Terrified, she gave in, unpigged my men and made a solemn promise—no more tricks. Circe kept her promise, and became our friend. We stayed for a whole year, and then it was time to go. "Fine," she said, "but before I can let you leave for Ithaca, you have to go to Hades and consult the dead." "What, the underworld?" I said. She gave us no choice, and so we set sail for the fog-shrouded edge of the world, the border of Hades.

Circe had told me how to raise the dead. I won't go into the messy details, but it involved sacrificing a couple of sheep, among other things. It worked. Thousands of droning spooks boiled out of the ground. Scary? Yes, but their conversation can be rather boring. One of the exceptions was the spirit of the blind prophet Tiresias, who gave me a heads-up about our journey back.

"There's good news and bad news," he said, spookily. "The island of Thrinacie lies on your route: the good news is that if you and your men *don't* eat the Sun-god's cattle there, you may all get home alive. The bad news is that if you *do* eat them, you've all had it. Even if you, King Odysseus, survive and get back, you'll find your palace full of scrounging Suitors, competing to marry Queen Penelope. You'll have to kill them all."

Heartbreakingly, I also saw the ghost of Anticlea—my mother. She had a message of hope, though. Penelope and my son Telemachus were still faithful to me and longed for my return! You don't linger in Hades unless you're a resident, so we boarded our ship and beat it back to Circe's island. Circe welcomed us with a feast. Then she told me about some of the upcoming highlights of the route home to Ithaca.

"First, you have to pass the Sirens," she said. "Two females, part human and part bird, crooning songs of delight and deep knowledge. Hear them, and you won't want to go home. Or, to be more accurate, you *won't* go home. Any sailor will dive overboard if he catches even a few notes from these charming songbirds. The Sirens sit next to a pile of skeletons, so you can guess what happens to all their fans."

Without Circe's warning, we would have been doomed. She told me to plug my sailors' ears with wax, so they wouldn't hear a thing. I could listen, but I would have to be tied tight to the mast, so that taking a swim was not an option. And that's how it happened. Ears firmly stoppered, my men rowed safely past the Sirens. I was roped to the mast, and listened to the most beautiful songs in the world, all the while desperate to plunge into the sea and strike out for the Sirens' fatal island.

Circe had also warned me about the next waypoint on the journey.

"You'll have to pass through a narrow sea channel running between Charybdis and Scylla. They're monsters. Charybdis sits in the deep. Three times a day she sucks in water, then blows it out again, creating a deadly whirlpool that will swallow any ship.

"Scylla is more visible than Charybdis, though her habits are no nicer. She lives in a cave on the other side of the channel. She has long necks and many heads, each with triple rows of teeth. She's immortal, she's invulnerable, she's not open to reason, and she likes to gobble up passing dolphins and sailors."

It was just as dangerous as Circe predicted. I warned my crew about the whirlpool, but not about Scylla. I was afraid that if they knew, they might stop rowing and hide below deck, leaving us to drift right into the whirlpool. We made it through in the end, but Scylla ate six of my men.

Circe's Sorcery

The god Hermes told me that the Moly flower would act as an antidote to Circe's sorcery. It proved to be a useful tip!

Find the path to Circe's house, collecting the Moly flower along the way. The Moly has six pink petals, a blue center, and two spiky leaves, and there is only one to be found.

He is
wearing
a patterned
cloak.

He is three
people north
of a man who
was killed
by an arrow.

Speaking with the Dead

The ghost of Tiresias had vital information about our
journey home, but where was he amid all these spooks?

Use the riddles of the dead to work
out what Tiresias looks like and find
out where he is.

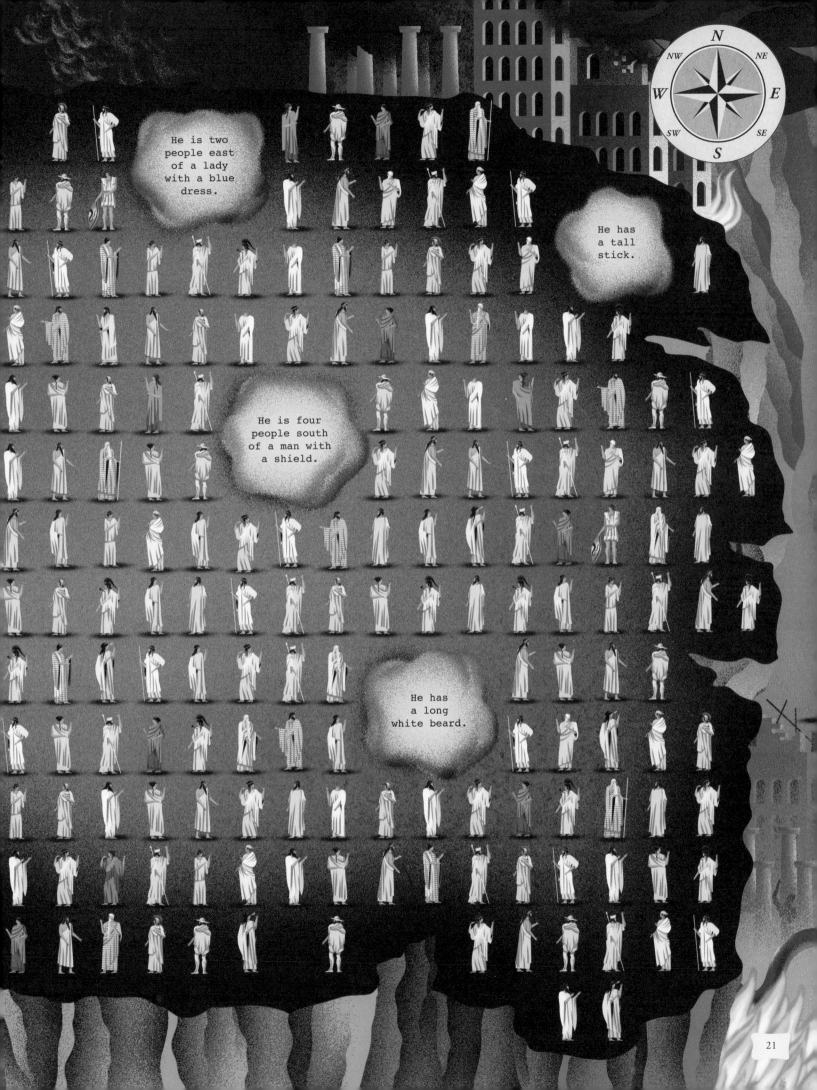

The Sirens' Song

Catch one note of this song, and you're dead.
Avoid hearing it at all costs!

Navigate the ship safely past
the Sirens and to the gap in
the rocks. The wind is strong
so, each time you move, you can
only travel exactly:
• Three squares south (S) OR
• Two squares west (W)
  or east (E) OR
• One square north west (NW)
  or north east (NE)
Do not move to a square with
musical notes or dangerous
rocks, and do not cross your
own path.

A Monstrous Choice

Scylla or Charybdis? Monster or whirlpool?
Lose some men, or lose all? That was my hard choice.

Every time you cross one of Scylla's heads, you lose a man. Lose more than six and you start again. Every time you cross a whirlpool, you lose the ship, and have to start again. Head for the sun on the horizon.

Return to Ithaca!

Then things got worse, if you can believe it. We reached Thrinacie, the isle of the Sun-god, but our food ran out. My men barbecued some of the god's cattle. Outraged that his pets had ended up as lunch, the Sun-god called on Zeus to punish us all. Zeus sent a storm that sank the ship, and drowned everyone but me. I drifted on some timber for nine days, and eventually washed up half-dead on Ogyia, the home of the goddess Calypso…

Calypso nursed me back to life and fell in love with me in the process, and could not bear to let me go. Grateful as I was, I could not love Calypso. My heart was set on returning to Penelope and Ithaca, so we lived in misery.

Thankfully, Athena now intervened, and persuaded Father Zeus to order Calypso to give me up. Calypso was distraught and bitter, but she still promised to do her best to see me on my way.

And she did. Calypso had no ship, but helped me to build a small vessel, using wood and other materials on the island. Brokenhearted, but true to her word, Calypso told me how to find Ithaca by following the stars, and then bade me a tearful farewell.

Eighteen days of solo voyaging followed. I was nearing the coast of Scheria, the land of the Phaeacians, but then Poseidon discovered where I was. The god had been away at a festival in Ethiopia, and returned to find *me* making *my* way across *his* waves. He unleashed a terrible storm. Mountainous waves threw me into the water, but once again, I was saved by goddesses. The goddess Ino rose up from the depths and told me to forget the ship and swim for Scheria. Then, Athena stepped in and calmed the storm, making it possible to swim.

Barely alive, at long last I staggered ashore on Scheria. Fortunately, Nausicaa, daughter of King Alcinous, found me and took me back to her father's palace. The Phaeacians were kindness itself. They fed and clothed me, and listened to my tale. One night, when I was in a deep sleep, King Alcinous even had me put aboard one of his ships and taken home.

Surprised and groggy, I awoke on a deserted beach. Well, not quite deserted—a young shepherd wandered over and told me where I was—*Ithaca*! At this point, the shepherd turned into a woman—it was bright-eyed Athena all along (confused? I was). She brought me up to speed on current events.

"Penelope and Telemachus remain faithful to you," she said, "but the Suitors are still competing to take your wife and your kingdom. You have to deal with them." Athena gave me a sneaky advantage and disguised me as a raggedy old man, to put the Suitors off their guard (I *so* love tricks). Then, before you could say "Mount Olympus," she zipped off to fetch Telemachus.

The disguise fooled my loyal old pig-herder Eumaeus, when I met him shortly afterwards. It even fooled Telemachus when he returned, but Athena made me reveal my true identity to him. We were both overjoyed to be reunited after so many years. Telemachus and I planned how to fight the Suitors, and he went off to the palace to prepare some weapons. I followed on with Eumaeus—who still thought I was just an old man. Once at the palace, only my old dog Argus recognized me—he got to his feet and wagged his tail, but the poor hound was very sick, and dropped dead with the effort. With tears in my eyes, and hardened bronze in my heart, I went inside the palace to reclaim my kingdom.

Not every Suitor was a villain, but all 108 of them were guilty in my eyes. For years, they had eaten me out of palace and home.

Hoping I was dead, they had schemed to marry Penelope and become king. Only her resourcefulness and her faith in my return had kept these freeloaders at bay.

Penelope didn't recognize the shabby old man who had entered her palace, however. Her brilliant mind was focused on resisting the Suitors, and she devised an impossible challenge for them. She set up a line of twelve ringed axes and said: "If any one of you can fire an arrow from Odysseus' bow through the rings on these axes, I will marry him."

Rightly, she guessed that the weedy Suitors wouldn't even be able to bend *my* bow to attach the bowstring. Each one failed. Then, I took a turn. I strung the bow and fired an arrow. Bullseye, times twelve! I shed my old-man disguise. Ever seen 108 faces go pale with fear simultaneously? They realized that Odysseus was back, and he was *not* in a forgiving mood. Aided by Telemachus, Eumaeus, *and* Athena, I attacked. We fought a fierce and bloody battle until every one of the Suitors lay dead.

Penelope is a *tough* lady, and even after all this she took some convincing that it really was me. When the truth hit home, it was like falling in love again—for both of us. Our nightmares were over. Well—not quite over. The relatives of the Suitors got an army together and marched on the palace, bent on revenge. Swords rang and more spears flew, until Athena stepped in and made peace.

Sailing by the Heavens

Calypso told me which way to steer by the stars, so I set off on my long solo voyage across the sea.

Navigate the boat to the coast of Scheria using the stars. Match the constellation on your current square to the star chart and travel one square north, south, east, or west.

Fooling People

I love tricks and disguises, don't you?
Athena's transformation had everyone fooled
as I made my way toward the palace.

Find your way to the center
of each maze and out again.
You'll need to pass Athena,
Eumaeus, and Telemachus, and speak
to them all before you finally
make it home to the palace.

Defeating the Suitors

The time had come for me to reclaim my palace and battle those scrounging Suitors—all 108 of them!

Find your way through my palace labyrinth to the Suitors in the main hall. Collect exactly 108 arrows by the time you reach them. You must collect the arrows in each room you enter. Do not pass through the

Farewell, traveler...

My battles and voyages done, I was finally reunited
with Penelope, Telemachus, and the people of Ithaca.
My voyage, my *odyssey*, was now truly at an end.

How about sailing off on your own odyssey, traveler?
May you have fair winds and a following sea, and
the bright-eyed goddess Athena to watch your back…

… AND ON *NO* ACCOUNT OFFEND
ANY OF THE GODS OR GODDESSES!!!

Answers

The Lotus Eaters

Tricking the Cyclops

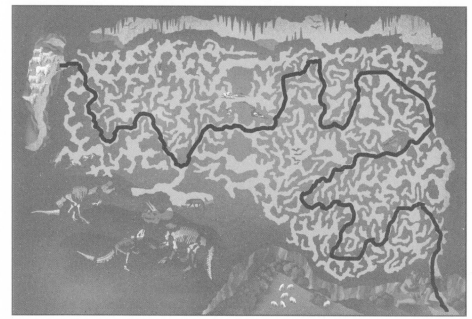

Attack of the Cannibals

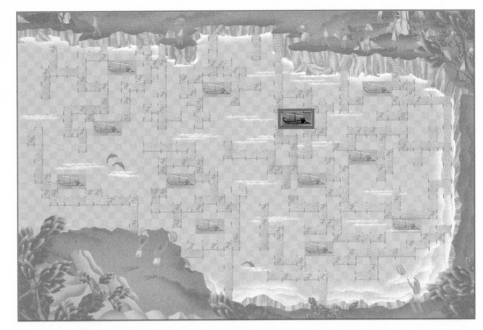

Circe's Sorcery

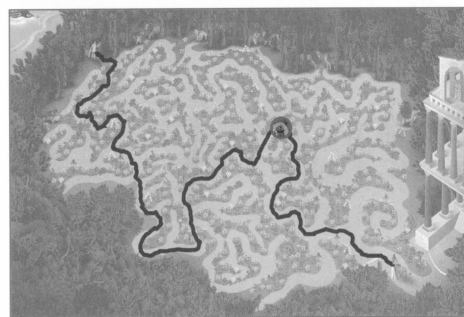

Speaking with the Dead

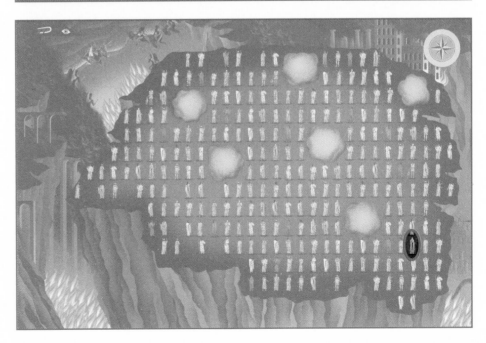

The Sirens' Song

A Monstrous Choice

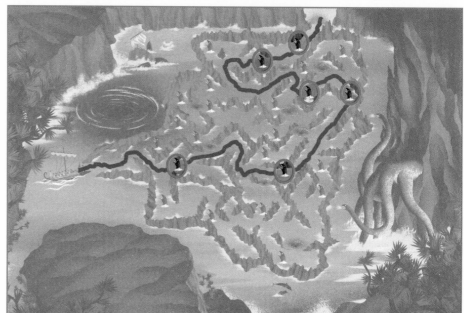

Sailing by the Heavens

Fooling People

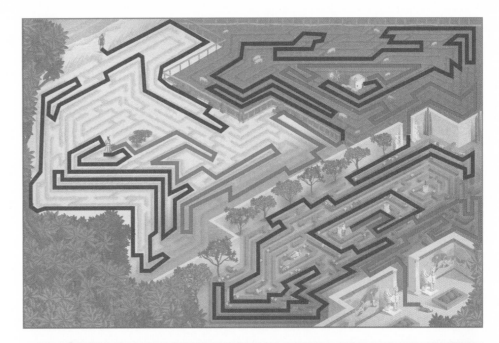

Defeating the Suitors

Homer and the *Odyssey*

It is thought that between about 750 and 650 BC, a Greek named Homer wrote two long poems, the *Iliad* and the *Odyssey*. The *Iliad* is about a short period toward the end of the Greeks' long war against Troy. The *Odyssey* is set in the ten years after the war, and tells of the wanderings of Odysseus, one of the Greek kings, as he tried to find his way home to Ithaca. Unfortunately, we know next to nothing about Homer. Homer was probably a man, and he may have lived on the coast of what is now western Turkey, but that is about it.

Some of the stories in the *Iliad* and the *Odyssey* may have started out as tales told by stand-up poets to live audiences, hundreds of years before anyone wrote them down. However, it looks as if at some point an author collected them, and then used his imagination to shape them into single stories. Homer's work helped to form the ideas of the ancient Greeks and Romans about religion, mythology, and art, and it has had a huge influence on Western culture ever since.